W9-AOU-523

The Canterbury Tales

Geoffrey Chaucer

Simplified by Michael West
Illustrated by Victor Ambrus

Longman

Longman Group UK Limited,
Longman House, Burnt Mill, Harlow,
Essex CM20 2JE, England
and Associated Companies throughout the world.

This simplified edition © Longman Group UK Limited 1987

First published 1987

ISBN 0-582-54150-6

Set in 12/14 point Linotron 202 Versailles
Produced by Longman Group (FE) Limited
Printed in Hong Kong

Acknowledgements

Illustrations from Canterbury Tales, edited by Geraldine
McCaughrean. Illustrations © Victor G Ambrus 1984 by
permission Oxford University Press.

The cover background is a wallpaper design called NUAGE,
courtesy of Osborne and Little plc.

Stage 2: 900 word vocabulary

Please look under *New words* at the back of this book
for explanations of words outside this stage.

Contents

Introduction

Geoffrey Chaucer

The writer of *The Canterbury Tales* was many other things besides a writer. He was not of high birth but his education and his powers of mind made him a very useful servant of the king.

We think he was born in London about 1340. So he would have been nineteen years old when he went to France with Edward III's army. He was taken prisoner by the French, but the king himself seems to have paid the ransom to free him.

After that, Chaucer did work of several kinds for the king and his ministers. Sometimes he was sent to other countries to speak for the king or the court. A visit of this kind to Italy in 1372–73 is probably important for us. He may have met Boccaccio himself, but he certainly became interested in the Italian story-tellers and poets. We can be sure he read Boccaccio's *Decameron* (1348–58).

We know that Chaucer planned his *Canterbury Tales* in 1386 or 1387. He wanted to have stories told by thirty pilgrims, but he was a very busy man, and the collection was unfinished when he died in 1400. He himself made a pilgrimage to Canterbury in 1388.

Geoffrey Chaucer was buried in Westminster Abbey. His is the earliest of the great names in "Poets' Corner" in the Abbey.

There is one more fact to remember. Printing, with movable metal type, was introduced in Germany about 1450. Caxton made the first printing press in England in 1477, and his press printed *The Canterbury Tales* in 1478. So Chaucer himself never saw any printed book of the kind we know today.

The Canterbury Tales

Chaucer's was not the first collection of short stories. It was not even a new idea to have a group of people each telling a story. In Boccaccio's *Decameron*, ten people have escaped to the country from the plague, a terrible illness, in Florence in 1348. They pass the time by telling stories.

Chaucer's *Canterbury Tales* also has a group of people each telling a story, but our interest is as much in the story-tellers as in the stories. Each of them is a real person. Chaucer introduces them in the Prologue, and then we meet them again between stories. Before long, we feel that we know them personally. We don't have pardoners and summoners today, but we all know people with characters just like the pardoner and the summoner.

The Tales are told (in Chaucer's book) in

poetry. Most of them are in "heroic couplets" – 10-syllable lines that rhyme in pairs (for example, *lyve* and *fyve* in the first two lines below). Here is the beginning of Chaucer's description of the Wife of Bath:

In Chaucer's English

She was a worthy womman al
    hir lyve:
Housbondes at chirche dore
    she hadde fyve,
And thries hadde she been at
    Jerusalem;

She hadde passed many a
    straunge strem;
At Rome she hadde been, and
    at Boloigne,
In Galice at Seint-Jame, and
    at Coloigne.

Modern English

She had been a respectable
    woman all her life.
She had been married in
    church to five husbands,
And she had been [on
    pilgrimage] to Jerusalem
    three times;

She had crossed many
    foreign rivers;
She had been to Rome, and to
    Bologna[1],
To Santiago de Compostela
    in Galicia[2] and to Cologne[3].

[1] on pilgrimage to the grave of St Dominic
[2] in Spain – the grave of St James the Greater
[3] in Germany – the remains of the Magi, the Three Wise Men

The Prologue
At the Tabard Inn

Pilgrims go to a place because they want to please God. Their journey – a pilgrimage – is often to a place where a saint once lived or died.

Thomas à Becket was a saint. He was killed in Canterbury Cathedral, the great old church in Canterbury. Very many pilgrims went to Canterbury to visit the cathedral.

This book tells the story of some pilgrims who went to Canterbury together. On the journey from London, they each told a story – a tale.

The pilgrims met at a house called the Tabard Inn in London. The host – the inn-keeper – was a fat man. He was very happy and full of good stories which made them laugh. The pilgrims had a very good meal with a lot of good food and drink.

After the meal, the host stood up and said, "I'm very pleased to meet you. I've never met such a happy company. We're all going to Canterbury. It's a long way, and you need something to keep you happy on the journey. Each of you must tell a story on the way. We will give a very good dinner to the pilgrim who tells the best story. Will you do that? Hold up your hands if you'll do it."

Two pilgrims on the way to Canterbury

The pilgrims all held up their hands. They cried, "Yes! Yes! We'll do that. And we'll make the host our leader. He will tell us which story is best."

The host made all the pilgrims get up very early next morning. They started on their journey. When they stopped to give their horses water, the host said, "You remember what we said last night about telling stories?"

"Yes," they said. "Who will tell the first story?"

The host said, "I will ask the knight to tell the first story."

The knight had just come back from the war. He was going to Canterbury to give thanks to God because he had come back safe and unhurt.

The Knight's Tale
Palamon and Arcite

Duke Theseus once ruled over Athens. He was a great soldier. He had conquered Scythia in a war, and he had married its Queen Hippolyta. When she came to live with him in Athens, she brought her younger sister, Emily, with her. As they were riding back to Athens a soldier brought bad news.

"Creon has begun a war against you, Duke Theseus. He has conquered Thebes."

Theseus sent some of his knights to Athens with Hippolyta and Emily. Then he went to Thebes with his other knights. He fought Creon and killed him.

There were two young knights among the many men who fought for Creon. Their names were Palamon and Arcite. They were wounded, but they were not dead. They were lying side by side. They had rich clothes; so they were taken to Duke Theseus.

The duke said, "Your families will pay a lot of gold if I set you free. But I will not set you free. You fought for Creon, so you will never be free again."

He sent them to Athens to be shut up as prisoners in a high tower.

Duke Theseus rode home and lived happily in Athens with Hippolyta and Emily.

Palamon and Arcite lived sadly in the high tower. One morning Palamon got up very early and looked out of the window into the duke's garden. He saw a lady. She was very beautiful. She was walking in the garden and putting flowers in her hair. This beautiful lady was Emily.

When Palamon saw her he gave a loud cry. Arcite heard him, and said, "Dear Palamon, what is the matter? Your face is white. Why did you cry out? Think! We are prisoners and we will always be prisoners. We must learn to bear this sad life quietly."

Palamon said, "I didn't cry out because we are prisoners. I cried out because I have just seen the most beautiful lady in the world. I pray to the gods to make me free. Then I can be with her. But, if I cannot be free, I want to die."

Arcite looked out of the window and saw Emily. He cried, "If she will not love me, I do not want to live any more."

This was too much for Palamon. He said, "We have been brothers in our sad life here, shut up away from the world. Now you want to steal my lady. You cannot do that! I loved her first and I will love her for ever. You must help me to win her."

Arcite said, "You saw her first, but I love her as much as you do. How can you *or* I win her when we are shut up here in this tower?"

Palamon said, "One day we may be free, and then let the best man win!"

For many days the old friendliness between them was quite lost.

Duke Theseus had a good friend, called Duke Perotheus. Perotheus had known Arcite for many years and liked him very much. He heard about Arcite in the tower. He said, "I'm very sorry to hear that Arcite is your prisoner. He's not like Creon. He's a good young man. Please let him be free. Please let Arcite come out into the world again."

Duke Theseus thought, "Perotheus is in my house. I like him and he has asked me to do something. It will please him if I do it."

So he answered, "Yes, Arcite can come out of the tower. He will be free. But he must go away from Athens, and he must never come here again. If he ever tries to come back I will cut off his head."

Before Arcite left prison, he had a last talk with Palamon. He said, "I must leave Athens, but you can stay here and look at my beautiful lady in the garden. It is better for you than for me."

Palamon was just as sad. "You will be free," he said. "Perhaps you will come back with an army and make war on Athens. If you win, my beautiful lady will be yours."

Life seemed very hard to both the young men.

Arcite was in Thebes, far away from Athens, but he still loved Emily. He thought of her every day. He became very ill.

One night, the god Mercury came to him in his sleep and said, "Go back to Athens. When you are in Athens you will be happy again."

Arcite sprang up and cried, "I will go back to Athens at once! If the duke catches me, he will cut off my head. But I am not afraid of death if I can see my beautiful lady."

He looked at his face in the glass. His illness had changed him very much.

"No one will know me now," he said. "I can go quite safely to Athens."

He went back to Athens and became one of the servants in the house of the Lady Emily. He got water; he cut wood; he was happy to do any hard work for her! He did well and at last he became her head servant. Everyone liked his quiet voice and his hard work and his goodness. They called him Philostrate.

Even Duke Theseus began to notice him. For seven years he became dearer and dearer to Theseus.

All this time, Palamon had lived his sad life in prison. He had no hope of getting out. His great love for Emily was making him ill. But at last, one night in May, a friend of Palamon put something in the drink of the man who kept watch over him. The man fell asleep; Palamon took his key, opened the great door, and was free at last.

He ran a long way, but the night was short. When the sun came up, Palamon hid in a little wood. His plan was to walk by night and hide by day.

He thought: "I will go back to Thebes. I will return at the head of an army. I will kill Theseus and win Emily."

The next morning, Arcite was riding along, singing in the sunshine. He got down from his horse, and he started to walk through the wood. Palamon was hiding there. Arcite sat down. He said, "Emily is still far away from me. I have in me the blood of kings, but I'm only a servant to Theseus. I'm not even called by my own name. My love for Emily makes me sad; all my sadness has come from my love for Emily."

When Palamon heard this, it was like a knife in his heart. His face grew as white as death. He sprang up. "Arcite!" he cried. "Now I know all about you! You were like a brother to me, but you love my lady. You or I must die. I have nothing to fight you with, but I'm not afraid. I am Palamon: I will kill you!"

Arcite answered quietly. "Do you not know that love is free? I tell you plainly, I will always love this lady. But we'll have a fair fight. Tomorrow, I'll meet you here. I'll bring a sword for you

8

and you can fight me with it. And tonight I'll bring you food and drink. Then you'll be strong for the battle. If you win, the lady will be yours."

Palamon answered, "I will be happy to fight you."

The next morning Arcite rode to the place of battle. Then the great fight began.

On the same May morning, Duke Theseus was riding in the wood with his wife, Hippolyta, and Emily. They heard the sound of fighting, and soon they saw the two knights.

Theseus rode his horse between them. He cried, "Stop! Why are you fighting like this, with no one to make sure that you fight fairly?"

Arcite was tired; he had lost hope. "Sir," he answered, "we are two unhappy men. You are our lord. Kill me first; then kill my friend."

Palamon said, "This is Arcite. By your order he must die if he is found in Athens. But he calls himself Philostrate, and he is your head servant. He has done all this for love of the Princess Emily. And I am Palamon. I have broken out of your prison. I too love Emily, and I will gladly die now, at her feet. Kill me, but kill Arcite too."

The duke answered, "Yes! You must both die."

But the queen and Emily and all the ladies with them began to cry. They said, "These two fine young men must not die!"

Then the ladies fell on their knees and asked

9

Emily with Palamon and Arcite

Duke Theseus to let Palamon and Arcite liv,
"Oh, let them live!"

The duke said, "The god of love is a great god.
These two young men could live safely like kings
in Thebes. Yet they are fighting against each
other here. They are doing this because they
both love the same girl. But she knows nothing
at all about it! Well, you shall live. But you must
promise me that you will never come and make
war on my land. You must be my friends
always."

"We promise," they said. "We will always be
your friends."

The duke then said, "Emily cannot marry both
of you. But I have a plan. Go home to Thebes.
Come back here in one year. Each of you must
bring a hundred knights, ready to fight for you.
The one who wins that battle shall marry Emily.
Do you like my plan?"

Both young men fell on their knees and
thanked him again and again. Then they went
home to Thebes. They began to get ready. Each
chose a hundred knights.

Duke Theseus, too, had many things to do. He
built a place outside Athens, ready for the battle.
It had stone walls, with white gates on the east
and west sides. The duke made three temples – a
temple of Venus the goddess of love, a temple of
Diana the goddess of outdoor life, and a temple
of Mars the god of fighting. There were beautiful

pictures in temple of Venus and a garden full of flowers. In the pictures Venus had roses on her head and a beautiful bird flying above her.

The temple of Diana was not like the temple of Venus. Venus wants everyone to love and to marry. Diana does not want people to fight or to marry. She wants them to be happy all day, and to ride in the fields. She loves the early morning; so in her temple there was a picture of the moon. It was just going and morning was coming.

The temple of Mars was not a happy place. It made everyone who saw it afraid. It had pictures of men fighting, and pictures of battles and burning towns. There was a picture of Mars with a fire burning in front of him.

Now the end of the year had come. Palamon and Arcite came back to Athens, each with his hundred knights. The two armies made a fine sight. Theseus himself came out to meet them.

Before the battle began, Palamon and Arcite each said, "Theseus has built temples near the battlefield. I must visit one of them."

Palamon thought, "If I pray to Venus, she will help me. I will ask her for a quick death if I don't win." So he prayed in the temple of Venus and she seemed to move her head. He cried, "The goddess moved her head! I am very happy. She will help me!"

Arcite went to the temple of Mars, the war god. He said, "Mars, help me to win the battle over Palamon!" When he had finished, the doors moved and a ringing sound came from Mars himself. The fire in front of the god burned up suddenly. Arcite heard a low voice saying, "You will win!"

But Emily did not want to marry. She loved to be free in the woods and the fields. So she went to the temple of Diana. She said to the goddess, "I do not want to marry either Palamon or Arcite. If I *must* marry, please let me marry the one who loves me most."

Diana would not listen to her prayer. The fire which burnt in front of Diana went out. Emily began to cry. Then the goddess herself stood before her. "Do not cry," she said. "The gods have said that you must marry one of these two men. Both have been very unhappy for you. But I cannot tell you which of them will marry you."

The god Mars and the goddess Venus quarrelled. Each had said that one of the two men would win, but only one of them could win.

Now you will hear how Mars and Venus each kept their promise.

Palamon and Arcite had come to Athens on a Sunday. All the people there ate and drank and sang and danced on Monday. Early on Tuesday everyone went to see the great fight.

It was a very fine sight. There were beautiful horses and brave men everywhere. There were lords and knights in fine clothes and ladies in beautiful dresses. Duke Theseus sat and watched it all.

A soldier came out and cried, "Listen to the duke's orders!" When they were all quiet, the soldier said, "Duke Theseus does not want anyone to die. No one will use a sword or anything with a dangerous point. Anyone who is hurt will be taken prisoner. If the leader of either side is taken, then the battle will end. Now let the battle begin!"

There was warlike music. The queen and all the lords and ladies, and Emily, rode out to watch.

Arcite came onto the battlefield by the western gate, near the temple of the god Mars; his clothes were all red. Palamon came by the eastern gate, near the temple of the goddess Venus; his clothes were all white.

It is hard to find words to tell about the great fight that followed. Horses fell and rose, and men fell.

From time to time servants brought food and drink to the fighters. The battle went on all day. Suddenly Palamon was taken prisoner. That was the end of the fight.

Duke Theseus said, "Arcite will have Emily. He has won her in this long day's battle!"

The people cried out, "Arcite! Arcite! Arcite is the winner!"

Before the battle, the goddess Venus had told

Palamon, "I will help you." So now she was unhappy. She went to her father, Saturn. Saturn listened to her. Then he said, "My dear daughter, it will be all right. Wait and see."

There was loud music as Arcite rode down the battlefield towards Emily. He looked up at her and she looked down at him. She thought, "He is a brave and beautiful young man! I believe I could love him and marry him!" Suddenly, something made his horse afraid. It sprang into the air and then it fell. Arcite was thrown to the ground. He lay still; his face was covered with blood. They carried him gently to Theseus' house and laid him on a bed.

The doctors came. At first they thought, "Arcite will not die." But Arcite's wounds became worse and worse. Then they said, "The wounds are too deep. He will die."

They told Arcite that he was going to die. Then he sent for Palamon and Emily. He said to Emily, "I have loved you so much. I have been unhappy because of you. Now I must lay down my life for you."

Then he turned to Palamon and said, "I have had much unhappiness because of you, but now death ends everything. Perhaps it is the best way." Then he turned to Emily and said, "Emily, if you want to be a wife, think of Palamon. Emily and Palamon! It will make me happy in the other world."

He closed his eyes. Death was near. His eyes became dark, but at the very end he looked up at Emily and said her name.

All the people of the city wept for Arcite for many days.

Time makes most things better. Months went by.

The people of Athens had often fought with the people of Thebes, but now they wanted to be friends. So Duke Theseus sent for Palamon.

Palamon came. He was wearing black clothes for his lost friend, Arcite. Then the duke said, "Put an end to your unhappiness. You will not forget Arcite, but you can still be happy. Don't you remember that Arcite said to Emily, 'If you want to be a wife, think of Palamon.' Does that not make you a little happier?"

The duke called for Emily and took her hand. "Sister," he said, "I will tell you the wish of all my people. If you love Palamon and marry him, then we in Athens will be friendly with the people of Thebes. Take good Palamon and marry him. He has loved you for a long time."

He said to Palamon, "Take this lady by the hand. She will be your own dear wife."

So Palamon and Emily were married and lived happily every after. The people of Athens and of Thebes were friends again.

All the pilgrims said, "That was a beautiful story."

"Yes," said the host. "We have made a good beginning."

Some pilgrims told other stories. Then the host turned to the Clerk of Oxford. He said, "You haven't said a word since we started. Perhaps you've been thinking about your books. Now think about us, and think of a good story to tell us."

The Clerk of Oxford was learning to be a priest. He loved books, and he also loved to teach people about the things that he read. He was very poor; his clothes were old and had many holes in them because he had no money. He and his horse never had enough food.

The Clerk's Tale
Patient Griselda

The clerk said, "My story is about a patient wife."

Once, in beautiful part of Italy, there lived a great lord, a marquis. His name was Walter. He was good to look at, and he was kind to poor people. He was young and strong, but he had no wife. This made his people very sad.

At last, they came to him, and they asked him to listen to them. A wise old man spoke for them all.

"Great marquis, we come to you because you are good. You will not be angry with us if we tell you what is in our hearts. Please take a wife. Then we will be happy. It is right for you to marry. You will have someone to love you and care for you. And you will have children."

Then the wise old man said, "If you wish, we will find a wife for you. She will be both beautiful and rich!"

Walter laughed at this, but he was pleased. He answered, "You know very well, my dear people, how much I like to be free. I do not want a wife, but perhaps, as you say, I should marry. So – yes, I will get married very soon. But I will find my wife for myself! And I ask you to treat my wife like a king's daughter. You must do this for me. I am doing a lot for you."

They said, "Yes, we will do that. We will treat her like a king's daughter."

So they went to their homes and waited for the day of the marriage. They were all very happy.

A very poor man lived not far from the great house of the marquis. His name was Janicula. All the people who lived near him were poor too. They lived in small huts and worked very hard in their little fields.

Janicula had a daughter. Her name was Griselda. She was beautiful, good and kind. She loved her old father and looked after him well. Walter had often seen her when she was doing her daily work. She looked after her father's few animals, and she was often outside the house in the wind and rain. She did not know that anyone ever watched her at work. But to Walter she was the most beautiful girl in the world.

"I could love her very much," he thought. "I have never seen any rich lady so beautiful and so good."

The day came for the marriage. But the people did not know about Griselda. The marquis had not told anyone about her.

The great house was very full. Many people had come from far and near to stay in it. The marquis had bought beautiful dresses and jewels. Everything was ready.

"Follow me," said the marquis to all the lords and ladies. He led the way out of his great house towards the little huts where some of his people lived.

The lords and ladies asked each other, "What is he going to do?" But they followed him.

That morning, Griselda finished all her work early so as to see the wife of the marquis. She thought, "If I stand with the other girls, I may see the rich and beautiful lady who is going to marry the marquis. First I will put my father to sit in the sun." She went to the door of their little house. She opened it. The marquis stood outside. In his beautiful clothes he looked like a king.

"Griselda," he said, "where is your father?" The old man came out, and Walter took him by the hand.

"Janicula," he said, "I must tell you what is in my heart. Please let your daughter be my wife, if she will marry me."

The old man was very surprised. He could not speak at first. Then he answered, "Yes – I must say yes if Griselda says yes."

"May I speak to her and to you, here in your house?" said the marquis quietly. "I will ask her if she will be my wife. She must promise always to do what I ask."

The people waited outside.

The marquis spoke gently to Griselda. "Griselda," he said, "your father says that we may marry. Please take me for your husband. But I must first ask you this. Will you promise always to do what I tell you to do?"

"My Lord," she said, "I am only a poor girl. You have asked me to be your wife. If you will let me look after my father in my new life, yes, I will marry you, and I will always do everything you tell me to do."

"That is enough, my dear Griselda," said Walter. He took her hand and led her out to all the waiting people. "Here is my wife," he said.

Some ladies came forward. They came into the little house and helped Griselda to wash. They had brought beautiful clothes for her, and Griselda put them on. They put a crown on her head.

When she came out of her hut, the people could not believe their eyes. They had never seen anyone so beautiful. The marquis was very happy. They were married that day, and there was music and dancing all night.

For a long time the marquis's country was happy. All the people loved Griselda, the daughter of Janicula. She helped the poor because she loved them. Everyone said, "The marquis did a wise and good thing when he married Griselda."

A little girl was born to Walter and Griselda. The people said, "One day this little girl will be as

21

beautiful as her mother."

Walter thought, "Griselda has a child. Will she be the same now? If I ask her to do something very hard, perhaps she will not do it."

Then Walter did something very bad. It is hard to believe it. Until now Griselda had done everything he wished, and he knew she loved him very much. But he went on with his bad plan.

He came to her one day with a hard look on his face.

"Griselda," he said, "when I married a poor man's daughter my people did not like it. Now you have a child and it is even worse for them. I will send a man to take the child away from you. You must let him do this. Remember your words on your marriage day!"

Griselda did not show her sadness. At first she said nothing. Then, at last, she said, "Both I and my child are yours. You can do anything with us."

The marquis was glad when she said this. He sent a man to Griselda. The man said, "My Lord says that I must take away this child." Then he caught up the little sleeping child in his great arms.

Griselda said, "Please let me kiss her before she goes away." She took her child, and she said quietly, "Goodbye, my daughter. I shall never see you again. May the good God take care of you."

As the man took her daughter away, she said,

The man takes Griselda's daughter away

"Please put her little body in the ground. It will be safe there from beasts and birds which may try to hurt it."

He brought the child to Walter. Walter said, "Take her to my sister in Bologna. Tell her to look after her well. Do not tell her that it is my child."

Walter watched Griselda. She seemed to love him in the same way. But she was very quiet and her face was often sad.

Then a little boy was born. Walter was glad, and his people were glad. They said, "This child is our prince. One day we shall be his people."

But after two happy years the same bad thought came to Walter. Walter was like some other people. He wanted to be sure about his loving and patient wife.

This time, he said the same thing as before, but he added, "My people do not want a grandson of Janicula for their prince. So, again, I order you to give your child to my man."

"My Lord," she answered, "I have always said that I will do everything that you tell me to do. Do what you wish with our son." Then she added, "I love you. If you will be happier without me, I will die to please you. Let me only keep your love."

Nothing changed the marquis's heart. He sent the same man to take away her little boy. Again, she asked only to kiss her son before he left her for ever. And she said, "Put his little body in the ground. Then no beast or bird can hurt it." Walter sent the little boy to his sister.

Again, Walter watched his wife, and again her patience and her love for him never changed. But the people were angry with the marquis. All over the country they said ugly things.

One said, "He has killed his two children! He did not want Lady Griselda to love the children. She must love only the marquis."

Another said, "And yet she never changes in her love for him, and she still cares for all of us when we are poor or ill!"

Now Walter did one last bad thing. He sent letters to Rome and got back some papers. These papers looked like real letters from the Pope, but they were not real letters. They only looked like real ones.

These papers told him, for the good of his people, to send his wife away. They told him to take a wife from some great and rich family.

The simple people were sad. They loved Griselda very much. But because they were simple, they believed Walter. They thought that the letters from Rome were real. "The marquis must send Griselda away, and he must marry again," they said sadly.

When Griselda heard about it, she thought, "This is the worst thing of all. I love my husband more than anything in the world. How can I ever live away from him?"

No one knew about it, but the marquis had sent a letter to his sister in Bologna. "Let your husband bring the two children to me. Tell no one who sent them to you. You must say, 'This little girl will be the wife of the marquis.'"

His sister's husband set out from Bologna with the two children, as the marquis asked. The little boy and girl were very beautiful. They were dressed in rich clothes and jewels, and they rode on fine horses.

But now the hardest time of all came for poor Griselda. One day, in a room full of people, the marquis said, "Well, Griselda, it wasn't a bad thing for me when I married you – you have been quite a good wife to me! It certainly wasn't a bad thing for you or for your old father! But now I must change my way of life. My people want me to send you away and to take another wife – a girl from a good family. The Pope has ordered me to do that. Be ready – my new young wife is now on her way here."

Griselda's answer moved the hearts of all who heard her. But she did not move the hard heart of her own husband.

"I am not good enough to be even your servant," she said. "I am certainly not good enough to be your wife. I have always known that. Thank you for the beautiful home that I have lived in for so long. I will gladly go back to my father now because you and the Pope want me to do that. I will never marry again: I will always love you – only you. You told me that you loved me, but the old saying is very true: 'As men grow old, love grows cold.' I must leave everything behind me here. I will take my old clothes to wear."

Her goodness and love almost made Walter cry. But in a hard voice he said, "Keep the clothes you are wearing. Yes, you may keep those."

Griselda took off all her jewels and her rich dress. She took even the shoes off her feet. She put on her poorest clothes. Then she began to walk home. Many people followed her and cried. But Griselda did not cry.

Her father had never liked her marriage. The marquis was too rich and high above them. Janicula asked "What has happened to Griselda's two children?" He tried to find out, but Griselda never told him. He had heard about the new wife who was soon to come for the marquis.

He saw his daughter coming and he ran out and took her in his arms. In every way he showed her how much he loved her and wanted to help her. For a time Griselda lived quietly with him. She worked in the little house and in the fields. It was like the old days.

But her husband still had not done enough. One day he sent for her. "Griselda," he said, "I wish to give my new wife the best things. You must help me. You know my house, and you are good at looking after me. You must now work for my new wife. You look very poor in that old dress, but I will take no notice. Please start work here at once, and make everything ready for my new wife."

Griselda was happy. "I shall be very glad if I can help you." And she began at once.

She put gold and silver on the big tables. She made all the beds. She washed the floors herself. She told the servants to be quick, and she herself worked fastest and best of them all.

At midday many people came to the house of the marquis to see his new wife. Griselda met the people and led them to their places. Then Walter showed them a beautiful young girl. He said, "Griselda, how do you like the beauty of my young wife?"

Griselda said, "I have never seen anyone more beautiful. I hope she and you will be happy together. But I ask this of you. Be kind to her. She was born of gentle people. She has been brought up as a lady. I was poor and I worked hard in my father's house. It will be harder for her. She cannot bear unkindness."

At last Walter knew that Griselda still loved him. "I have been very bad," he said to himself. "I have hurt Griselda, but she still loves me."

"It is enough, my dearest Griselda!" he cried. "I will never hurt you again or bring sadness to you. Now I know how good you are and how patient you are, and how true you are to me." He took her in his arms and kissed her again and again.

He told her everything. And then he said, "This is your daughter." And he led the young girl up to her. "She is our daughter. I was not really going to marry her. This is our son. I sent them to Bologna. They have been safe and well all these years."

Griselda was very happy. She called her children to her, put her arms round them and kissed them both. Many people who were watching began to cry.

"Oh, thank you!" she said to Walter. "Thank you for saving my children for me. I can die now. I have both them and your love!"

Her ladies took Griselda to her own rooms. They took off her old clothes and put her rich clothes on her. With her crown on her head she went to take her place for ever as Walter's wife.

They lived happily for many years. They married their daughter to a very rich and very good man. The marquis gave old Janicula a room in his house. Their son became marquis when his father died.

"That," said the clerk, "is the end of my story. All wives should not try to be as patient as Griselda. That would not be good."

At the end of the clerk's story Chaucer wrote: "Patient Griselda is now dead, so I may say openly to all husbands: Do not try the patience of your wives and hope to find them like Griselda. They will certainly not be like her!

"And I will say something to all wives: Don't be afraid of your husbands. Even if your husband is big and strong, your words will always win in a battle."

The Wife of Bath's Tale
What do women want most?

There were only a few women among the pilgrims who were riding to Canterbury. One of them was the Wife of Bath. She was a large woman with a red face. She wore a big hat, and she rode on a very fat horse. She was rich, and she had travelled far and wide in the world. She had had five husbands, but they had all died. She liked to talk and be happy. Her tale was about the time of King Arthur and his Knights of the Round Table.

Once there was a young knight. He had done a very bad thing: he had broken the laws which all knights must keep.

King Arthur heard what the young knight had done. "That is very bad!" he said. "He must die."

The queen and her ladies were sad because they liked the young knight very much. "He is not really bad," they said to each other.

"Please, please," they asked the king, "please do not end this young man's life. He knows that he has done a bad thing; he will never make such a mistake again."

The king said to the queen, "Well, do whatever you like with him. But he must pay for breaking the law."

The queen thought for a little time; then she said to the knight, "You shall live, if you can tell me the answer to this question: What does a woman want most of all? I will give you a year and a day to find out the answer. If you cannot find it, you must die."

The knight thanked her, but he rode away very sadly.

He said, "The queen has asked a very hard question. How can I find the answer?"

He asked many people, "What does a woman want most of all?"

He got many answers.

A man said, "Women like jewels and money more than anything else."

One woman said, "What do women want most of all? They want to be happy. That's what they want."

"What do women want most of all?" said another woman. "Fine clothes, of course. That's what they want."

He asked some children.

A little girl said, "My mother is most happy when she's cooking good food for us."

A little boy said, "My mother likes best to have a new baby in our family."

"Our mother is happiest of all when she sees our father come home at night," said two or three children all together.

Many of the answers seemed very good answers, but none of them seemed to be right. There was no answer that *everybody* said was right.

At last a year had passed. The knight had to go back and take his answer to the queen.

The poor knight thought, "What shall I say? What can I say? I have tried so hard! Must I really die?"

Just then he came to a great wood. Twenty-four beautiful ladies were dancing there on the green grass. He said, "Here are twenty-four more people that I can ask. I have just enough time to ask them."

He turned his horse towards them . . . Where were they? They had all gone, suddenly, into the air! Only one very old, very ugly woman sat there now. When he came near, she stood up and came to him.

"Sir Knight," she said, "are you looking for something? Tell me what it is, and perhaps I can help you. We old people are wise; we know many things."

He said, "You may be just the person who can help me. I will lose my life if I cannot find the answer to a question: What does a woman want most of all? If you can tell me, I will pay you well."

"Give me your hand," she answered. "You must do the first thing that I ask you. Promise!

Then I will tell you the right answer."

The knight said, "I promise to do the first thing that you ask me to do."

"Then your life is safe," said the old woman. "Not one person – not even the queen – will say that your answer is not the true one."

She spoke very quietly into his ear. "That," she said, "is the answer to your question."

Then they went along together to meet the queen and all the lords and ladies.

The people heard that the young knight was coming. Everyone went to tell everyone else and they ran to the meeting-place. The queen was there, ready to hear his answer. Many men and women were afraid. "The young knight will die," they said.

"It was a very hard question," they said to each other. "It will be bad if he cannot tell the queen the answer."

Everyone became quiet as they stood around. They heard the queen say in a clear voice, "Now can you tell us, Sir Knight, what a woman wants most of all?"

The knight came forward. He fell on his knees in front of her. Everyone heard his answer.

"My lady and my queen, the thing which every woman wants most of all is to be head of her house. She wants to make her husband do as she wishes."

When they heard this, all the people said that it was the right answer! "Let him live!" they cried.

The queen was very pleased with this answer. She said, "You shall be free, and live!"

Suddenly, the old woman came forward. "Be good to me too, my lady," she said to the queen. "I said to the knight, 'I will tell you the answer, but you must promise to do what I ask you to do.'" She turned to the knight. "Didn't you promise that?"

"Yes," said the knight. "That is what I promised."

She said, "I ask you to take me as your wife." Her face was very ugly. It was uglier than ever!

The knight said unhappily, "What you say is true. I did promise. But please – please let me go free! Don't make me marry you!"

"No!" she said. "No! I am old and ugly and very poor, but I want most of all to be your wife. I want to win your love."

"My love!" he answered. "You cannot really hope for that!"

The queen and her ladies and the people were laughing. They knew that the knight wanted to die now. He did not want to marry this ugly old woman.

Then the queen spoke: "You must do as you promised."

"Yes," said the knight, "I must do as I promised. I must marry her."

There was no dancing and singing; there were no fine clothes and fine food, no jewels and flowers at their marriage. It was done very quietly.

Then the knight went away and hid for the rest of the day. He did not want to look at his ugly old wife.

That night, his ugly wife turned to him and said, "Come, dear husband. Is this how a Knight of King Arthur keeps his promise? What have I done wrong? Tell me, and I will try to do better and please you."

"Do better?" said the knight. "You cannot make your age less and you cannot make your face any better."

"Is that all that is wrong?" she asked, laughing at him.

"Isn't it enough?" he answered.

"Beauty is only on the outside," she said. "The face becomes old but the heart is always young. What a person does is the great thing. The man who does the best and kindest things is far better than a great lord who does bad and unkind things."

For a long time, she talked quietly to him. He was surprised. "You know a great deal, and you are very good," he said. "You've taught me a lot about men and women and goodness and badness."

The knight and his new wife

At the end she said, "Is it better to have a wife with a beautiful face who gives you great unhappiness? Or a wife who is old and ugly but is very kind to you and makes you very happy?"

The knight's heart was softened by all he had heard from her.

"My lady, my love, and my dear wife," he said, "you are very wise and good. I will do what seems best to you."

She laughed. "Remember the answer which you gave to the queen? Will you let me rule over you?"

"Yes, truly," he said. "I know it will be best."

She kissed him and said, "Don't be angry. I will be both to you – both beautiful and good. If I am not as beautiful as any queen tomorrow, do as you wish with me!"

And the knight drew her to him and kissed her. And he found that he was kissing a very beautiful girl – the most beautiful girl in the world. For his wife was really a fairy. She had wanted to see if he was a good knight.

They lived happily together all their lives.

That is the end of my story. May God send us husbands who are young and loving, and may we be able to make them do whatever we wish. Men should do what their wives tell them to do. And they should not be too careful with their money.

The Pardoner's Tale
Three men looking for Death

"I speak in churches," said the pardoner. "I always speak about the same thing. I say in Latin, *Radix malorum est cupiditas*. That means, 'The love of money is the cause of all evil.' It is the cause of all wrong-doing and of all the bad things which can happen to a man.

I sell pardons – things which make God forgive men. God will then pardon them for any evil which they have done.

"After I've spoken to the people, I bring out my things. These are bones or bits of cloth or other things. I say that they have belonged to saints, but I don't really know that. People believe me and so I get money from them. I tell the people that the love of money is the cause of all evil, but I do all this in order to get money. I don't live like a poor man. Oh no! I must have good clothes and good food. The poor people give me the money to buy these things. I sell them pardons, and so they are happy."

The pardoner's story is a very good story. It is surprising for a bad man to tell such a good story.

This was the story.

39

There were three young men who did very many bad and foolish things. They drank too much, and they did no work. They tried to get money in evil ways.

While they were sitting drinking one morning, they heard a bell. It was ringing in front of the body of a dead man.

A boy had just brought them more to drink. They asked the boy, "Whose body is that?"

"He was a friend of yours," said the boy. He was killed last night while he was drinking here. He was killed by that quiet thief called Death. Death kills all the people in this country. Death killed your friend and went away. He has killed thousands and thousands of people. You should get ready to meet Death."

"I am not afraid to meet him!" cried one of the three young men. Then he jumped up. "I'll find him! I'll look for him in every field and wood and town. Listen!" he cried to the other two. "Let's hold up our hands and promise to be brothers, and we'll find and kill Death because Death has killed so many of our friends."

"I'll go with you," said the second man.

"And so will I," said the third man. They had both already drunk a great deal.

They said, "We will kill this dangerous person called Death, before night comes."

So they went off at once to find him.

They walked a little way, and they saw an old man. The old man spoke to them kindly. He said,

40

The three friends see the old man

"God be with you, my young friends."

But the young men were not at all kind. They said, "Old fool! Why is your ugly body covered with all these clothes?"

He said, "I am very old. I feel the cold. I cannot get warm."

They answered, "Why have you lived so long, you ugly old man? Why don't you die?"

The old man looked at them angrily. He said, "I live like this because I cannot find any young man who will change with me. No young man wants to become old. So I must become older and older. Death will not come and take me, so I go up and down the country. I am an unhappy traveller looking for Death. I say to the ground under my feet: 'Dear Mother Earth, let me come in! Oh, Mother Earth, I want to lay myself down in you and rest for ever!' But she will not be kind to me. That is why I am old – so very old."

He had not finished. He drew his old body up and said quietly to them, "But you speak very unkindly to me, and that is a very bad thing. I have done nothing to hurt you. You should speak more kindly to an old man. I have no more to say. I must go on with my long journey to meet Death."

One of the young men laughed. "No, you can't do that!" he shouted. "You have just spoken about Death. He has killed all our friends in this country. Now we are going to kill him. Tell us where he is."

The old man said, "Don't speak like that. If you really want to find Death, I can tell you which way to go. Turn up this little lane. Not long ago I saw him sitting by a tree in that wood. He will not be afraid of anything that you can do. He is there, by that great tree. You are foolish to think that you can save men from Death. May God help you to become better men."

The three young men turned and ran towards the tree he had shown them. There was no one there. But on the ground they saw a great number of golden coins. They were very pleased to see all this money. They did not remember that they were trying to find Death.

But Death was very near, and he was thinking about them.

They sat down with all the gold; they put their hands into it and let the gold pieces run through their fingers. They sat there for some time and did not speak. At last one of them spoke. He was the young man with the most evil heart.

"Listen to me," he said. "This money will give us happiness for the rest of our lives! We must not take it away in daylight because people will think that we're thieves. One of us will go back to the town for food and drink. The two others will hide in this wood and watch the money until night comes."

This plan seemed good to the others. They

sent the youngest man to the town to buy food and drink.

As soon as he was out of sight, the first man said to the other, "We are like brothers – as we said. But one of us is gone now. Take half of this gold for yourself, and I'll take half for myself."

The second man said, "How can we do that? Our young brother knows all about the gold! There are three of us."

"I'll tell you how we can do it. There are two of us. Two men are stronger than one. When the boy comes back, we'll play a game with him, a game of fighting. You can start a playful fight with him. I'll watch for a good opening and I'll drive my knife into him. After that, my dear brother, there will be all this gold for only us two – half of it for you, and half for me."

And so they planned death for their young friend.

But the young friend was bad too. As he walked to the town his mind was full of those beautiful pieces of gold. He said to himself, "I must make a plan to get all the gold for myself. Then I will be the happiest man in the world!"

At last he said, "I know what I'll do!" He went to a shop and said, "The rats are eating the corn on my farm. I haven't even got enough corn to make bread. Give me something to put in the rats' food to kill them."

The man in the shop gave him a small bottle

of poison. He said, "This will kill your rats. Put it in their food or drinking-water. It is so strong that it will kill any living thing in the world."

Then the young man went on to the next street and he bought three bottles of wine. He put the poison into two of the bottles. He kept the third bottle for himself. He said, "I shall need this bottle of wine after I have killed my two friends. I shall need to drink after I have worked all night carrying away the gold and hiding it."

Then he bought some food and went back to the other two men. They said, "Ha! He's bringing us our evening meal but he'll never eat it! He doesn't know what we will do to him!"

They sat down to eat the food. Then the two men killed the youngest man.

Then they said, "Let's eat and drink before we put his body in the ground."

One man took up a bottle of wine. He drank a lot of it and gave the bottle to the other man.

They both died in great pain.

They had come out to kill Death, but Death came and found them all dead.

And Death laughed!

"That is the end of my story," said the pardoner. "Now I have some things here in my bag. They will bring forgiveness to you and they will save you from evil. Only a penny! Come and buy!"

The Franklin's Tale
Three promises

The franklin was a rich farmer. He had a big house and a lot of land. He liked good food and wine. People who came to his home always had nice things to eat and drink. He told a story about three promises.

Long ago, in France, a knight called Arveragus loved a lady called Dorigen. She wanted to be sure that he was brave and good, so she asked him to do many hard things. "This will show how much you love me," she said.

He went away and had many adventures. He did all the hard things that she had asked. Then he came back to her.

She said, "Now I know that you are not afraid of anything. I love you as much as you love me. I want to marry you."

He loved her very much. He said, "When we're married, I will never ask you to do anything that you don't want to do."

"And when we're married," she said, "I will be your good and loving wife. I shall never do anything that will make us unhappy."

They went to Arveragus's home in Brittany and lived lovingly together for more than a year.

But the knight had always been a man of war. Even his happiness with Dorigen could not keep him from his love of fighting. He wanted to go to England and fight there.

So he sailed away for two whole years.

Poor Dorigen was left at home. She could not be happy. She loved her husband very much. She could not sleep; she could not eat.

Her friends tried hard to help her.

They said, "You will die if you don't try to sleep more and eat more."

She got better very slowly. She was young and full of hope. "My husband will come back again," she said.

Arveragus sent her letters. "All is well," he said in his letters. "I will be home again soon."

Her friends said to her, "Now you are feeling better, so you must come out of your house. Don't sit alone any more. Come and be with us." So she began to go for walks with them.

As she walked by the sea with her friends, she saw the great black rocks in the sea. They made her feel very afraid. Sometimes, away from the sea, she lay on the grass and thought about them.

She thought: "I don't like rocks. They can kill men when they sail near the land in their ships. Why did God make them? Why did God make something which can kill men? He loves all men!"

Her friends saw that she was becoming ill

again. They were kind people. They kept her away from the black rocks. They took her out to dance, and to play games with them.

One day in spring, they went to a beautiful garden. They sat down on the grass; then they danced and sang. Only Dorigen was unhappy. She saw so many men dancing happily, but none of them was Arveragus.

One of the dancers in the garden was a young man called Aurelius. He was a fine young man. He had loved Dorigen with all his heart for two years. But he had never said a word to her about it. Some of his friends knew that he was in love, but they did not know who the lady was.

Now Aurelius could no longer keep his love hidden in his heart.

He said to her, "I know that your heart is over the sea with Arveragus. You are the wife of another man. I know that you cannot love me, but I love you deeply."

Dorigen did not like to hear this.

"You must never say such things to me again, Aurelius. I could never leave Arveragus."

Then she said, laughing, "Aurelius, I will love you if you can take away all the rocks from the sea. Then Arveragus can come safely home in his ship."

"Is there no other way than this?" he asked.

She answered, "No, there is no other way."

Aurelius went away. First he prayed to the

Aurelius tells Dorigen that he loves her

Sun God: "O Lord of the Sun, I pray you to speak to your sister, the Moon. Ask her to make the sea rise up higher and higher and cover the rocks. Then my lady will love me! She must do what she has promised."

But nothing happened. The sea did not rise and cover the rocks. He became very ill. His brother came to take care of him. Aurelius told him everything. "I must make those rocks go," he said. "If they go away, I shall be a very happy man."

His brother was a man who had read many books. He wanted to help Aurelius.

Two years passed. Then Arveragus came home from the wars. He had done very well and he had fought bravely. Dorigen was very happy. All their friends were very happy. Only Aurelius knew nothing about it. He lay at home, very ill. His brother stayed close to him. He read his books and thought all the time about his brother Aurelius's wish. "How can I help Aurelius?" he asked himself.

At last he remembered something. "One day in Orleans, I saw a book in a friend's house. It was a book about magic. If I can get that book it will tell me how to make those rocks go. Even if they are hidden only for a little time, that will be enough to give my brother his wish."

He told Aurelius about this book. Aurelius listened to him and felt better. He jumped out of bed. In a day or two he was much better. So he went to Orleans with his brother.

As they came near Orleans, they met a young man. He was a magician. He said to them, "I know why you have come here." To their great surprise, he told them everything that was in their minds.

They went with him to his house that night. Before they ate, he showed them many strange things. They were all done by magic. Forests came before their eyes, full of animals. Then they saw a river, running through the room in which they were all sitting. They saw many knights fighting. The young man even showed Aurelius his love, Dorigen. Aurelius seemed to be dancing with her.

But all the time, they had not left the house.

Before they went to bed, Aurelius had made up his mind.

He said to the young man, "If you can take those rocks away or hide them, I will pay you a thousand pounds."

Next morning they all rode to Brittany. It was December, and it was very cold. At once the magician set to work. He began to make magic.

The sea rose up and covered the rocks. Not one rock could be seen.

Aurelius went to Dorigen. He told her once more how much he loved her. He ended, "Do as you please, but think of what you said in the garden that day. I have done what you told me to do. All the rocks have gone."

He went away and left her.

Dorigen went down to the sea. She said, "It is true! All the rocks have gone – or the sea has come up and hidden them. Aurelius has done what I said. But what can I do now? Must I keep my promise? – or not?"

Arveragus had gone away for a few days. So she could not tell him about it.

She lay on her bed. She said, "What can I do? – Shall I kill myself? Other women have killed themselves because their husbands did not love them, but Arveragus loves me. Women have killed themselves because they loved a man who was not their husband. I don't love Aurelius. But I have made a promise. I must keep my promise. But I cannot keep it. What can I do?"

She lay on her bed and cried.

After two days Arveragus came home. He asked, "Why are you crying?"

Dorigen told him the whole story.

He looked lovingly at her. "Is that all?" he said. "Is there nothing more?"

"Is that not enough? What must I do?"

He said, "A promise is a promise. You must keep your promise. I love you very much, but I cannot love you so well if you break a promise. Truth is the greatest thing in the world. We must be true to ourselves and true to others. You must keep your promise."

Dorigen said, "I must go to the garden where Aurelius first told me of his love. He will go there, too."

Aurelius was going to the garden where he had first told Dorigen about his love for her. On his way to the garden, he met Dorigen in the street. Aurelius was full of happiness. But Dorigen's eyes were red with weeping.

Aurelius said, "Where are you going?"

She said, "My husband has told me that I must keep my promise. I'm going to the garden where first I met you. I'm going to keep my promise."

Aurelius looked at Dorigen. He saw how sad she was. He thought, "I am doing a very bad thing. I'm asking her to be untrue to her husband Arveragus. She loves him very much." He said, "Tell your husband Arveragus that I can see how good he is. I will not come between his love and you. You are the best and truest wife I have ever met."

Dorigen fell on her knees to thank him. Then, with a heart full of happiness, she went home to her husband. For the rest of their long life together he cared for her like a queen, and she was always his true and most loving wife.

Poor Aurelius began to think, "How can I ever pay the magician all that money? I will have to sell all that I have. And, even then, I won't have enough. Perhaps he will let me pay something every year."

He found that he had five hundred pounds. He took it to the magician and said, "Here is all my money. I will get all the rest of the money for you. But please let me have two or three years to get the money and pay you."

The magician said, "I did what I promised to do. You promised to pay me a thousand pounds."

"Yes," said Aurelius. "You did what you promised and I promised to pay you."

"Haven't you had the love of your lady?"

"No," said Aurelius. "No, I have not. Her husband loved her very much but he wouldn't let her break her promise. So he sent her to me. When she said, 'Take away the rocks and I promise to be your lover,' she did not know the kind of magic that you can do. How could I make the poor lady keep her promise? I sent her back to her husband."

The magician said, "My dear brother, you have done the right thing. And now I will do the right thing. I won't take any of your money. Goodbye. I wish you well."

He got on his horse and rode away.

The franklin's tale was ended. "My friends," he said, "now you must tell me the truth. Which of those three men seemed the best man to you? – Aurelius? – or Arveragus? – or the magician?"

The Friar's Tale
The summoner and the devil

Among the pilgrims there were two men who hated each other. One was a summoner and the other was a friar. A summoner calls people to go before a high officer of the Church when they have done some wrong. A friar asks people for money for the Church. The summoner often got money because he promised not to tell about people's wrong-doing.

The friar hated the summoner and he said to the pilgrims, "I'm going to tell a story about summoners." The summoner said, "I'll tell a story about friars." But the friar said, "I will tell my story first."

So the friar began.

There was once an archdeacon – a great man in the Church. He was a bad man. If people gave him money, he let them do whatever they wanted.

A summoner worked for him. This man watched people quietly. He caught them when they did bad things. Then he said to them, "You must leave the Church. We won't let you come into the church to pray if you don't give me money."

One day he was going to see an old woman. She believed that she had done something bad. And he wanted to make her pay him money. On the way he met a man.

"Where are you riding to?" asked the man.

No one liked summoners, so the summoner made up an answer. "I'm just going to get some money that an old woman near here must pay to my lord."

"Oh, then you are a bailiff," said the man. A bailiff is a man who looks after land for the owner of the land. He goes to the farmers who work on the land and gets money from them. They pay him because they use the owner's land.

"Yes," answered the summoner, "that's what I am. I'm a bailiff."

The man said, "I have a farm. I look after it for its owner. Let us be friends."

The summoner answered, "Yes. I do work like that. Tell me, how do you get money from people?"

The man said, "I like a lot of money, but my master does not pay me enough, so I have to get it in other ways. I take whatever anyone gives me!"

The summoner said, "That is true of me, too. I must make people give me money. I have my own ways of doing it. I don't mind if it makes them sad or afraid. I think we are like each other! So it's time we learnt each other's names."

The man asks the summoner to be friends with him

The man's answer gave him a surprise. He said, "I will tell you who I am. I am a devil. I live in hell."

"I thought you were a man like me," said the summoner. "You look like a man."

"We can look like anything we want to," answered the devil. "There are good reasons why we have this power. Now – let us go on our travels."

They started off. They saw a man with a cart which was so heavy that his horses could not pull it along. He was hitting the horses and shouting at them.

"The devil take you!" he cried. "The devil take you and the cart, too!"

The summoner said to the devil, "Did you hear that? Why don't you go and take his horses and cart? He says that you can take them."

The devil answered, "You cannot believe all that you hear. Wait and see what happens."

The horses pulled harder and harder; the cart began to move. "Good horses!" the carter shouted. "Well done, Brock! Well done, Scottie! God save you all!"

"What did I tell you?" said the devil. "He said one thing but he meant something else. There is nothing for me here. We must go on."

When they had left the town behind, the summoner said to the devil, "You didn't do very well with the man and his horses. Now I'm going to get some money from this poor old woman. Watch carefully and see how I do it."

He went to the old woman's door. "Come on out!" he cried. "I'm sure you're doing something bad!"

"Who is that?" said the old woman. "Oh, God be with you, sir."

The summoner said, "Go to see the bishop. People are saying some bad things about you. You must say if they are true. If they are true, you must pay money to the bishop."

The old woman began to cry. "Be kind to me, good sir," she said. "I am ill; I cannot get so far. Can I not pay you?"

"Yes, but you must pay me at once," said the summoner. "It will cost you twelve pennies. Be quick!"

"Twelve pennies!" cried the old woman. "Oh, help me, God! I don't have that much money. What can I do?"

"If I let you go free, may the devil come and take me away!" said the summoner. "Come on, pay up!"

"But I have done nothing bad," said the poor woman.

"Pay up, or I will take your cooking-pot. You were untrue to your husband. You know that you were!"

"I was never untrue to my husband. I loved him too much. As for you and my cooking-pot –

may the blackest devil in hell carry you off, and the cooking-pot, too!"

Now the devil spoke to her. "Do you really mean what you're saying?"

"The devil can do as I say," she answered. "He can carry him off – clothes, cooking-pot, and all!"

The summoner was still shouting at her. He was very angry. "Will I get no money at all from this old woman?"

"Why are you so angry?" asked the devil. "You and the pot are mine. She gave them to me. Tonight you will be in hell with me. There you can learn all that you want to know about us devils and how we do our work."

The devil sprang at the summoner and caught him. Then he carried him down to hell, where there is a place kept for summoners. It is always very full!

The friar had finished. He looked at all the pilgrims and said, "Think about my story, and may God keep us all from the devil who tries to catch us and take us down to hell!"

The summoner then told his story about the friar. But it was not a nice story. So I have not put it in this book.

The Nun's Priest's Tale
Chaunticleer and the fox

The nun who was going on the pilgrimage was named Madame Eglantine. A priest went with her to help her in her prayers. He was the nun's priest. His name was John.

The knight said, "We have had enough sad stories. Let's have a happy story."

The host turned to the nun's priest. He said, "Come here, priest. Come here, Sir John. Tell us a story that will make us feel happy."

The nun's priest said, "I will do my best." So he told the story of Chaunticleer and Pertelote.

Chaunticleer was a cock, and Pertelote was a hen.

This is the story.

There was a poor old woman who lived in a small house near a field. There was a wood near the house.

The old woman was so poor that she could not buy food. She ate only the things that she grew in her garden, and the eggs which she got from her hens, and she drank the milk from her cow.

The hens lived in her garden during the day. Chaunticleer, the cock, was the lord and master of the hens. Chaunticleer means "Sing beautiful-ly". Chaunticleer had a beautiful voice. Every morning he sang when the sun came up, and he sang every hour during the day. So the old woman could always tell the time by Chaunti-cleer.

Chaunticleer was lord over seven hens. But his wife, whom he loved most, was named Perte-lote. She was very wise and she knew her husband very well. He told her everything. And they sang love songs together.

At night Chaunticleer and the hens slept on the top of the old woman's house.

One morning, just before the sun rose, Chaunti-cleer was sitting on the top of the old woman's house with Pertelote and the other hens. Chaun-ticleer was making a loud sad noise, like some-one who is very afraid. When Pertelote heard him, she was afraid, too. She said, "Oh, dear heart! What is the matter with you? What a bad sleeper you are!"

"Don't be angry with me, my love," answered her husband. "I have had a very bad dream. I thought that I was in great danger. I am still afraid. May God make my dream bring me something good and not evil or danger."

"What was your dream?" asked Pertelote. "Tell me about it."

"I dreamt that I was walking in our garden. I saw a beast like a dog. It wanted to kill me! Its colour was between yellow and red. The ends of its ears were black. It had two burning eyes. I have never felt so afraid. That was the reason why I made those noises in my sleep."

"Oh!" said Pertelote, "I thought that I had a brave husband! Now I find that you are not brave. You are not the sort of husband that a woman wants. How can a brave man be afraid of dreams? Your dreams have come because you have eaten too much."

Pertelote knew a lot about the body. She was as good as any doctor.

She said, "You are ill. Your face is too red. There is too much redness in your blood. That makes people dream about fire and danger. When we fly down to the ground this morning, I will show you some plants. You must eat those plants and they will make you well."

She went on talking about different plants for different illnesses.

Chaunticleer was not pleased with all this talk. He did not like his wife telling him what to do. "Dreams mean something," he thought. "They are not caused by eating too much."

He said, "I thank you for your lesson, but perhaps you don't know that there are many wise and learned books about dreams. These books show that dreams have a meaning. Bad dreams may tell us of danger. I can tell you many stories about dreams that were true."

Chaunticleer was a great talker, and he really

Chaunticleer

had read a great many books. He told his wife about three dreams which came true.

Two men wanted to go on a pilgrimage. They came to a town where there were very many people. There were very few houses in which they could sleep. So the two friends had to sleep in different houses. One friend slept in a good house. The other man slept in a farm house.

The man in the good house dreamt that his friend was calling him. His friend was crying, "Oh, help me! Help me! I am in a room above a lot of cows. I am going to be killed. Come quickly!"

The friend had the same dream three times.

The third time, the man said, "It's too late. They have hidden my body in a farm cart. Go to the west gate of the town. You will find the farm cart there. My body is hidden under some earth in the cart."

So the friend went to the west gate, and there he found the body hidden on the cart.

Chaunticleer said, "You can learn from this story that dreams have a meaning. I will tell you another story – Two men wanted to cross the sea. They had to wait until the wind was just right.

"These two men slept in the city, ready to sail early on the next day. They went to bed in the same room, happy and pleased that they could sail on the next day.

"But listen, Pertelote. Something happened to one of them. In the night he dreamt that he saw a man in their room. This man said to him, 'If you sail tomorrow, you will die. Stay here, in this city, for one more day. Then you will be safe.'

"The man woke and told his friend the story. His friend laughed at him; he would not believe him. 'All right!' he said, 'I see that you want to stay here. You will lose the right wind. Dreams mean nothing at all. Goodbye!'

"He walked away. The man never saw his friend again. The ship sailed on to some rocks, and all the men in it were killed."

Chaunticleer told another story. It was about the son of the King of Mercia. The little boy was only seven years old. He dreamt that he was in danger. He told this to a kind woman who looked after him. No one believed the story. But his sister later killed the boy.

As Chaunticleer ended his three stories, he said, "I feel better now. My dear Pertelote, you are so beautiful that you make me feel well again. All my fears have gone. I feel much happier now."

They both flew down into the garden. Chaunticleer called all his hens to him and they began to eat. He was like a king among his hens. He was not afraid any more.

It was time for him to sing. So he lifted up his voice and sang. He made the noise of a happy cock. He was pleased to be as good as a clock for everyone near and far.

It was a beautiful morning.

"Madam Pertelote," he said, "hear how beautifully all these happy birds are singing. See how the flowers are coming up after their long winter sleep. Really, my heart is full of happiness!"

But just then a terrible thing happened. Our happiness in this world never lasts very long.

A fox had lived for three years in the little wood near the old woman's house. He came into her garden during the night. He was in the garden where Chaunticleer and his hens walked together. He lay there very quietly, hiding among the plants until it was midday. "That is the best time to catch poor Chaunticleer," he said to himself.

Oh, Chaunticleer, what a bad day it was for you! You came down from the safe house into the garden! What a bad morning it was for you! You thought that you could put your dream out of your mind!

It was a mistake for Chaunticleer to believe his wife. Women often make mistakes! I am a nun's priest, so I must not say too much against women.

Pertelote was happy sitting in a hole in the ground. All her sisters were round her. The sun was bright. Chaunticleer was near them singing loudly.

Then Chaunticleer turned and looked. He saw the fox. He stopped singing. He was afraid. He had never seen a fox before, but he felt that this was an enemy. He was just going to fly away when the fox said, "Dear sir, why do you want to fly away from me? I am your friend. I do not want to hurt you. I only want to hear you sing. You sing very beautifully. Your father (God rest him!) and your mother have both been in my house. It was very kind of them to come. I was very happy to have them there.

"I have never heard anyone sing so well as your father did on that morning! To make his voice even stronger he shut his eyes and stood up as high as he could. Now, please, sir, can you sing for me as your father did?"

Chaunticleer did not see the fox's true meaning. He was very pleased by the fox's words. He stood up as high as he could. He held up his head and shut his eyes and began to sing.

The fox caught him and threw him on his back. Then he ran with him towards the wood.

The hens saw the fox carrying off their beautiful cock. They made a terrible noise. Pertelote cried out louder than any of them.

The woman and her two daughters ran out of the house. They cried out "Fox! Fox!" and ran after them. The seven hens ran. People ran out of their houses and threw things at the fox. Three dogs ran with them. The cow ran. Ducks flew up from the ground. Even the bees went after the fox.

Everyone followed the fox and poor Chaunticleer. The women shouted "Fox! Fox!" The hens ran – *"Cluck! Cluck!"* The dogs ran – *"Wuff! Wuff!"* The cow ran – *"Moo! Moo!"* The ducks flew – *"Quack! Quack!"* And the bees came out – *"Buzz, Buzz."*

"Now good people," said the nun's priest, "you must listen to the end of my story. Then you will learn something."

Chaunticleer spoke to the fox. He said, "Sir Fox, you must turn round and say to those foolish people, 'Go back home! I have safely reached the wood. I shall eat this cock, and you can't do anything about it. So stop making that noise and go home!'"

The fox answered, "That's just what I will do." Of course he opened his mouth when he spoke. So Chaunticleer got out of his mouth and flew up into a high tree.

The fox looked up and said, "Oh, dear Sir Chaunticleer, I didn't mean to make you afraid of me. I didn't really want to eat you. Come down and I'll tell you the truth."

"No!" said Chaunticleer. "I will certainly not come down. I have been very foolish."

"Ah!" said the fox. "I was the foolish one. I talked. I must learn to keep my mouth shut."

"So," said the nun's priest, "be careful not to believe all the nice things that are said to you in this world. My story is not just a simple one about a fox and a cock and seven hens. It can teach you things. You can learn from it.

"And," said the nun's priest, "I pray to God to make us all good men and women."

Then the host said, "Thank you, Sir Priest. Thank you for a very good story."

At the end of his book, *The Canterbury Tales*, Chaucer wrote, "I pray that all those people who have read this book have liked it. And, if there were parts which you did not like, I ask you to think, 'He tried to do his best. He would have done better if he could.'"

Questions

Questions on each story

The Prologue
1 Where did the pilgrims in Chaucer's story meet?
2 Who wanted the pilgrims to tell stories?
3 Who had to judge the best story?

The Knight's Tale
1 What city did Theseus come from?
2 Who saw Emily first, Palamon or Arcite?
3 How did Palamon get out of prison?
4 What was Arcite's new name?
5 What was Mars the god of?

The Clerk's Tale
1 What country did this happen in?
2 What did the marquis ask Griselda to promise?
3 Where did he send their daughter?
4 Who brought the two children to the marquis?
5 Who was the marquis's "new wife"?

The Wife of Bath's Tale
1 How long did the queen allow the knight?
2 Who thought women liked jewels and money best?
3 Who told the knight the right answer?
4 What was the knight's promise to the old woman?
5 What was the right answer?

The Pardoner's Tale
1 Who went to kill Death?
2 Who told them where to find Death?
3 What did the youngest man go to the town for?
4 Where did he put the poison?
5 What happened to him in the end?

The Franklin's Tale
1 Why did Arveragus go to England?
2 What happened when Aurelius prayed to the Sun god?
3 Where did Aurelius and his brother meet the magician?
4 Who told Dorigen to keep her promise?
5 What had Aurelius promised the magician?

The Friar's Tale
1 Why did the friar tell a story about summoners?
2 What was the man that the summoner met really?
3 Why didn't he carry off the horses and cart?
4 Why did the summoner go to the old woman's house?
5 What happened to the summoner in the end?

The Nun's Priest's Tale
1 Why was the nun's priest going to Canterbury?
2 How many hens did Chaunticleer rule?
3 Where did Chaunticleer and the hens sleep?
4 How many stories did Chaunticleer tell?
5 What foolish thing did the fox do?